Fablesauce

FABLESAUCE

Aesop reinterpreted in rhymed couplets by

Pat Lessie

Haley's
Athol, Massachusetts

International Standard Book Number (ISBN): 1-884540-46-5

Haley's
Post Office Box 248
Athol, Massachusetts 01331
1.800.215.8805

Book design by Karen Gaudette in collaboration with
Pat Lessie and Marcia Gagliardi.
Copy edited by Helen Hills.
Printed by the Highland Press.

Library of Congress Cataloging in Publishing Data
Lessie, Pat, 1940-
Fablesauce : Aesop reinterpreted in rhymed couplets / by Pat Lessie.
p. cm.
Summary; Nine of Aesop's fables reinterpreted in rhymed iambic tetrameter.
ISBN 1-884540-48-1 -- ISBN 1-884540-46-5 (trade paper)
1. Animals--Juvenile poetry. 2. Children's poetry, American. 3. Aesop's fables--Adaptations. 4. Fables, Greek--Adaptations. [Animals--Poetry. 2. American poetry. 3. Fables. 4. Folklore.] I. Title.

PS3562.E839 F33 1999
811'.54--dc21 99-045092

For Edgar

Contents

What A Delight

a foreword by Lisa Wenner

There are some kinds of books librarians can't find enough of—among them are literate yet entertaining books of poetry for children. How lucky for us, then, that Pat Lessie has written *Fablesauce,* a book of rhyming fables. What a delight it will be for children and adults to discover this lively, rollicking collection of fables. Aesop has never been so entertaining.

Pat has culled the kernel of the fable and ripened it to full flavor in each of the nine tales she tells. Each of her animals presents the fullness of its animal self and, at the same time, reminds us of our human strengths and foibles. In "Lion and Mouse," she develops a contrast between carnivore and herbivore. The animal lion

> . . . dreamed of family feasts
> on antelopes and wildebeests.

As for the animal mouse, she tells us,

> Mostly Mousy gathered seeds
> and bits of fruits and tender weeds.

Personified, the mighty become weak and the weak, mighty. Human traits amplify the lion's demeanor:

> The lion, chuckling, set him free.
> He wouldn't need this mouse, not he,
> the king of beasts, so proud, so strong,
> so self-sufficient, never wrong.

When caught in a net, the lion again behaves in notably human ways:

> The lion thrashed, the lion screamed,
> while from his eyes big teardrops streamed.

Here is an opportunity for Mousy's character, human and admirable, to emerge:

> The tiny mouse retained his wits;
> he hadn't time for tizzy fits.
> He knew he'd have to gnaw the net.
> He didn't hesitate or fret.

Pat retains the fable's possibilities for moral consideration.

The small Meekins Library in Williamsburg, Massachusetts, where I am librarian, also serves as the local elementary school library. Shelves are jam-packed with stories waiting to be discovered. As we work with students, helping them move forward in their discovery of language, words, story, and rhyme, we want to present enthusiasm for our subjects and respect for our young readers and their intelligence. *Fablesauce,* like the best poetry for children, will both challenge and entertain its readers.

Pat Lessie is one of my favorite teachers. When I worked with her, she taught fifth and sixth grade. She always called before a visit to the library, often beginning her call, "Say. I have an idea." She knew that the books we push students to read often remain unread. Library visits for her students became voyages of discovery where avenues into various genres of literature were presented and then left open for children to discover on their own.

Each year, Pat spent time teaching poetry. She knew early on that listening to others read was the way some children came to an appreciation of words and their power. Children and adults will certainly enjoy reading these fables aloud to each other.

Fablesauce, with its charming scratchboard illustrations by Karen Gaudette, combines poetry, fable, and witty writing to several advantages. It is a handsome little book with pungent couplets, provocative moral considerations, economical and elegant narrative, and fine teaching potential. What more could you ask?

Embellishing the Time-Honored

an introduction by Pat Lessie

Yes, my parents did read to my sisters and me. I have vivid recollections of fairy tales, *Aesop's Fables*, and E. B. White's *Stuart Little*. The first chapter books that I read over and over by myself were the Thornton Burgess books about the animals inhabiting the world of the Green Meadows, the Smiling Pool, and the Laughing Brook. I loved animal stories. I am still fascinated by the fantastic creatures and plants around us. Undoubtedly this interest influenced my choice to study biology in college.

Many of us have warm memories of treasured family customs. When I was young my father started writing small poems, mostly couplets, on cards for packages he gave my mother on holidays. The poems gave hints about what was in the packages. My mother tried hard to guess before unwrapping them. Eventually, the custom spread so that several family members followed his example.

In their later years my parents have entertained guests by reading them an after-dinner selection, often light verse from Ogden Nash. When my father retired, he also wrote longer verses for birthdays and, now and then, a rhyming account of something that had happened to him. My favorite told of his car stalling in a low spot on a road in Tucson during a flash flood.

After my children grew up I became an elementary school teacher. I have enjoyed reading poems to my students and helping them learn to write in various poetic styles. Roald Dahl's book *Revolting Rhymes* has been very popular in my classes. His hilarious poems are spoofs of familiar fairy tales.

Several years ago, like my father, I reached a time in life when I had a little leisure and a desire to write creatively. I thought about putting stories into light verse, using couplets and a simple meter. I like the almost musical feeling that verse adds to a text. The stories I chose were fables attributed to Aesop, a Greek slave thought to have lived about 600 B.C.E. His characters are most often animals that talk and behave like people. Aesop used human characteristics to illustrate a moral in each brief, often humorous, tale.

In his book *Rhyme Stew* Roald Dahl also put one of the fables, "The Tortoise and the Hare," into verse. My version, "Hare and Tortoise," was written in the same meter and rhyme pattern. However, the two plots are quite different.

In my rhyming renditions of nine fables, I updated language and occasionally embellished time-honored versions with spicy dialogue. I took great freedom with the original story lines, adding details to make characters more realistic for today's readers.

It is my hope that these rhyming fables will amuse both children and the adults who read to them. I would be delighted if middle school students enjoyed reading them and adults entertained their dinner guests with one or two.

Now, hardly had Crow disappeared,
when, from nearby, a hare appeared.

Old Lion

A lion that could hunt no more,
since age had made him slow and sore,
decided that without his health,
survival must depend on stealth.
He chose a cave, lay down alone,
and there began to wail and moan.
The walls enhanced the mournful sound
so it was heard by all around.

A crow that had a kindly side
flew to the cave and stopped outside.
"Mr. Lion, are you ill?
I'm small, but I can help you still."
Sizing up the little bird,
"I just need company," he purred.
"Come, pass a little time with me.
We'll have a cookie and some tea."
In went the crow, and not one caw
escaped before the lion's paw,
in one enormous, crushing blow,
just flattened that misguided crow.
Down Lion's throat in just a flick
went Crow, the victim of the trick.

Now, hardly had Crow disappeared,
when, from nearby, a hare appeared.
The lion gave a piteous sigh.
The hare, though hesitant and shy,
queried, "Lion, are you cold?"
And Lion murmured, "No, just old
and suffering from a case of gout.
Come nearer, for I cannot shout."
The hare, with just a little doubt,
approached. Then—*thwack!*—the lion's clout
caught the creature unaware
and quickly squashed the timid hare.

Now, ask yourself, can this be fair?
Enticing victims to one's lair?
Devouring those whose sympathy
then draws them near? This should not be!
The other side, of course, is just
that to survive, the lion must
somehow obtain the food he'd need—
a clear necessity, not greed.

Next day, a young and frisky sheep
romped by the cave. She made a leap
that landed her on rocks up high.
She heard the lion's groans nearby.

The lion spotted her at play
and thought, of course, "Oh, lucky day!"
He called out softly, "Please come by
to visit me, for truly, I
am dying, and I'm terrified."
The sheep, thus caught off guard, complied.
And for this gesture, being nice,
she paid the price—her sacrifice.
(Even now this makes me weep,
for I am very fond of sheep.)

The next day, one young goat became
the victim of the lion's game.
And on this went a few days more
until a fox came. As before,
Old Lion called, "Please, come in, Fox,
for I'm too old to go on walks,
and I am lonely. Don't be rude.
Come, talk with me." But Fox was shrewd.
"Old Lion, sir, I heard you say
that you are in a sorry way.
And I was tempted to come in
to comfort you, though we're not kin,
until I saw the footprints here.
But what I noticed made me fear.

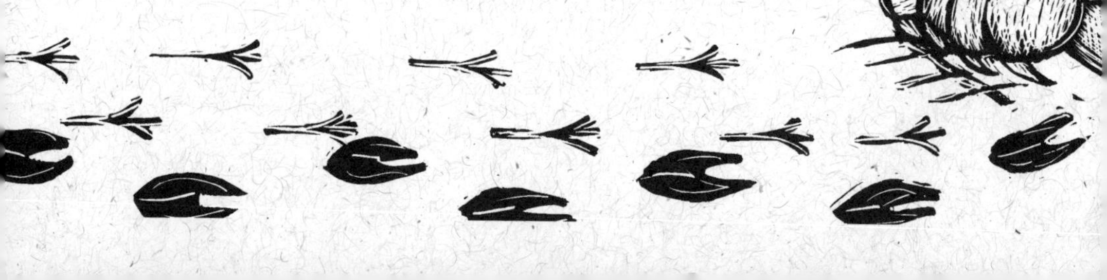

The prints all point in just one way.
They show that those who enter, stay.
I'll not fall victim to your con."
Fox turned and in a wink had gone.

Owl chose a hollow—the best one there.
The view was good, the space just fit
for one small owl to sleep or sit.

Owl and Grasshopper

A young owl pleased herself when she
found some hollows in a tree
adjacent to a farmer's field,
a field with such a bounteous yield
that, in among the stalks of wheat,
would be her grocery, complete
with chipmunks, gophers, rats, and mice,
plus voles and toads. "How very nice,"
Owl thought. Then, with the utmost care,
Owl chose a hollow—the best one there.
The view was good, the space just fit
for one small owl to sleep or sit.
She tidied it, but soon was done
in time to beat the rising sun.

Now owls, by habit, hunt at night
and slumber through the hours of light.
So when, beneath her all day long,
she heard a loud grasshopper song
(the chirping sound, like bow on string—
in this case rubbing leg on wing),
the owl pleaded, "Go away,
and let me get some sleep today."

With no reply she tried once more,
"Be quiet, Hopper, I implore."
Then, soon again, "Please, Mr. Hopper,
now some thoughtfulness is proper."

But Hoppergrass, the maddening twerp,
increased the volume of his chirp
'til, finally, Owl couldn't stand
much more of it, and so she planned
to terminate this chirping pest;
until then she would get no rest.

The fiendish plan she had in mind
started with her being kind.
"Hopper, sir, your song's so sweet
that neither harps nor flutes compete—
the tone, the tenderness, the skill,
the way you stridulate your trill.
I find your song leaves me awake,
so at this moment I'll partake
of nectar from a flower—the best
I've had. Please come and be my guest."

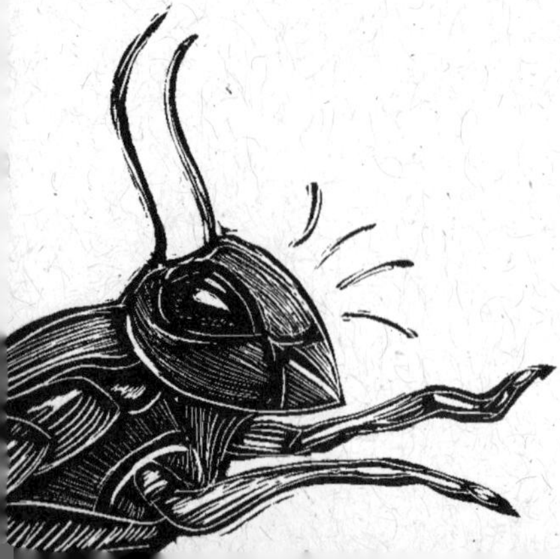

Thus praised so by the wily bird,
this hoppergrass, this little nerd,
with mouth now watering at the thought
of nectar, did what he should not.

Had Hoppergrass just thought it through,
considered Owl's intentions, too,
he would have seen he shouldn't go
to visit such a deadly foe.
But, putting common sense aside,
he let desire override
his judgment, choosing in some haste
to gratify his sugar taste.

"I'd be delighted," Hopper said.
"I'll come, but you go on ahead
to show the way, and I will follow."
Soon they were inside the hollow.
The hopper had no time to think,
much less to taste the nectar drink.
The young owl pounced
with strong, sharp claws,
placed Hoppergrass right in her jaws.

Owl gulped him quickly—one, two, three—
then rocked her head in obvious glee.

He made a meal, though really small,
for bugs aren't very big at all.
(Remember owls regurgitate
the tougher parts of what they ate,
so some of Hopper's parts came out
in pellet form, without a doubt.)
And as for that annoying chirp—
all gone. It didn't cause one burp.

Owl settled down in pure delight
to hunting critters every night
on big, soft wings in silent flight.
She slumbered when the day brought light.

The wily fox just had a hunch
that he would have that cheese for lunch.

Crow and Fox

This story from across the seas
concerns a crow, who stole some cheese
from Granny's kitchen window sill.
Crow held it tightly in her bill.
And also, it's about a fox
who dealt a lot with crows and cocks.

The crow took refuge in a pine.
She settled down, prepared to dine.
Meanwhile, Foxy, just below,
caught sight of both the cheese and crow.
The wily fox just had a hunch
that he would have that cheese for lunch.
Wasting little time or thought,
the clever fox conceived his plot.

He called up from beneath the tree,
"Oh, gorgeous bird above, I see,
when sunlight strikes your shiny plumes,
a radiant meadow filled with blooms
of gold and red, blue, purple, white.
Your feathers gleam with shades so bright.

Your wings must fly at eagle's pace.
Your neck is swanlike in its grace.
And if your voice is half as sweet
as you are fair, none could compete.
I'd be the happiest fox around
if I could hear your glorious sound."

The crow, thus flattered, gave a caw.
The cheese fell into Foxy's jaw.
He savored it, enjoyed the taste,
and Foxy didn't leave in haste.
First he told the somber crow,
"You are a pretty bird, you know,
and actually your caw, your voice,
is strong, although it's not my choice
for loveliness. But what you lack,
what really, really sets you back
is brains—you simply have no wits;
or, one might say, your mind's the pits."

Finished, Foxy disappeared,
feeling satisfied and cheered.
The crow, upset at what he'd said
about her empty, witless head,
remembered to her dying day
to weigh with doubt what foxes say.

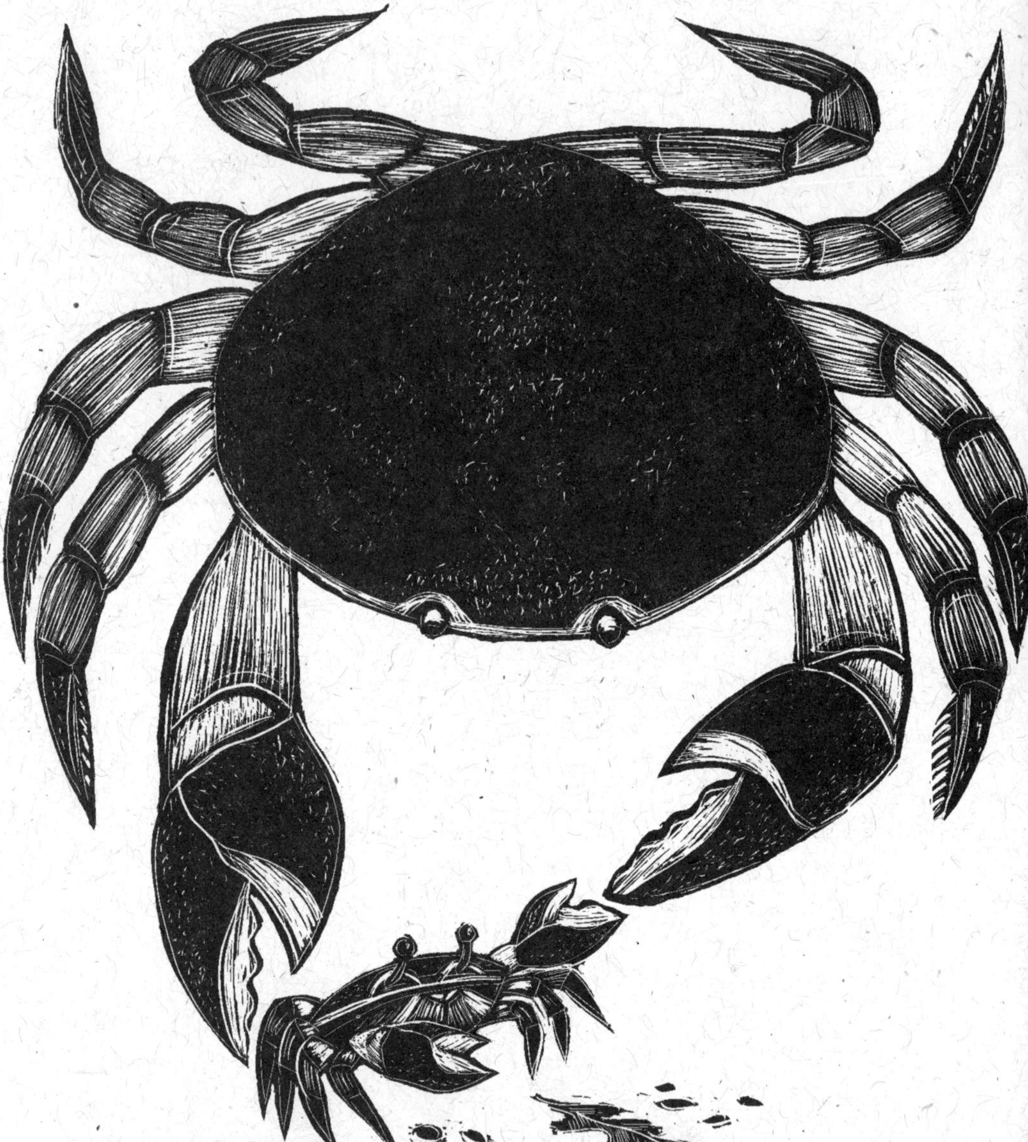

To please his mom, small Crabbie tried
to change from side to forward stride.

Crab and His Mother

Said Mama to her little crab,
"Son, please don't take this as a jab;
I can't abide your sideways gait.
Please practice walking forward—straight.
I know that this may be a strain.
We've got ten legs. Though eight are plain,
the pincers on the other two
are hard to balance. That is true.
But, be an athlete, be a jock.
Perfect the proper forward walk."

To please his mom, small Crabbie tried
to change from side to forward stride.
The youngster pondered if perchance
he could concoct a special dance
to train his feet to go that way.
The task could actually be play.
And so he spread his legs out wide,
then took one left, one right step-glide.
Next, three quick steps—a tiny run—
a sort of tango. It was fun!
But what he saw next dashed his pride;
he'd moved not straight, but to the side.

Crab coached himself, "Legs, form a huddle.
Now here's the plan; it's nothing subtle.
Work as a team, cooperate.
Now go, legs, go! Go forward—straight!"

While some legs did, some legs did not.
Disappointed, Crabbie thought,
"Mom's off her nut! This is no fun,
and, furthermore, it can't be done.
Besides, I really don't recall
a forward-walking crab at all!"

Some more attempts to change his course
failed, too, when Crabbie couldn't force
his legs to go the way they "should."
And so he called, "Mom, if you could,
just show me how this walk is done.
I'll learn your methods—every one."

Now on the spot, Mom tried in vain
to demonstrate, at least explain.
Finally, she lost her cool.
Admittedly she felt a fool
for knocking Crabbie, making mock
of Crabbie's standard, sideways walk.

And when this incident was done,
they both agreed, Mom and her son,
that one should never talk the talk
without the means to walk the walk.

"I'll race you then," the tortoise said,
"and at the end, I'll be ahead."

Hare and Tortoise

This tells a tale about a hare,
a cocky sort, and hard to bear
for one old tortoise, very slow,
but steady (as you surely know).
Now tortoises are never racy.
This one was a little spacy.
The bragging hare loved making fun
of Tortie, as he'd always done.
But teasing went too far one day,
with taunts that started out as play.
"You pokey thing, you dawdling clod,
you hardly move, the way you plod.
A race with you would be a snap,
even if I took a nap."

"I'll race you then," the tortoise said,
"and at the end, I'll be ahead."
It didn't take the hare a minute.
He accepted, sure he'd win it.
They both agreed a friendly fox
should choose the path with fewest rocks,
then pick a place where they'd begin,
and mark the finish line with "WIN!"

Soon "On your mark!" then "Start!" Fox said.
At once, the hare was far ahead.
There he maintained a steady stride,
which was, of course, a source of pride.
The day was fair. The sun was hot.
The hare was confident and thought
that, since he led by such a lot,
there was no way that he'd be caught.
He stopped to rest beneath a tree,
and put his head upon his knee.
In an instant (as you guessed),
the hare relaxed. In fact this rest
became an overpowering sleep,
the kind of slumber that's so deep
the hare would totally forget
about a challenge, race, or bet.

The tortoise didn't skip a beat.
He just kept moving all four feet.
On and on the tortoise trudged.
He passed the hare who never budged.
Some pebbles on the path were rough,
and though old Tortie's feet were tough,
thoughts must've danced inside his head
of swimming in a pond, instead.
And then, to boot, he scraped his shin,
but Tortie wasn't giving in.

The sun was really getting hot.
The tortoise, now, was quite distraught,
when, in the distance, up ahead,
he saw the sign, and clearly read
the fox's "WIN!" And Tortie thought
that, now, if ever, he should trot.
Trotting's not a tortoise gait,
but, sometimes, by a stroke of fate,
a thing not possible is done
as in this case. The tortoise won!

The crowd around him raised a cheer,
a cheer the sleeping hare could hear.
The hare, awakened, in a flash
began a frantic hopping dash.
But at the finish line, disgrace
was clearly seen upon his face.
To heap more hurt upon his shame,
for quite some time the hare was lame.
(In fact the hare was really wretched—
before the dash he hadn't stretched.)
The tortoise, on the other hand,
became a legend in the land.

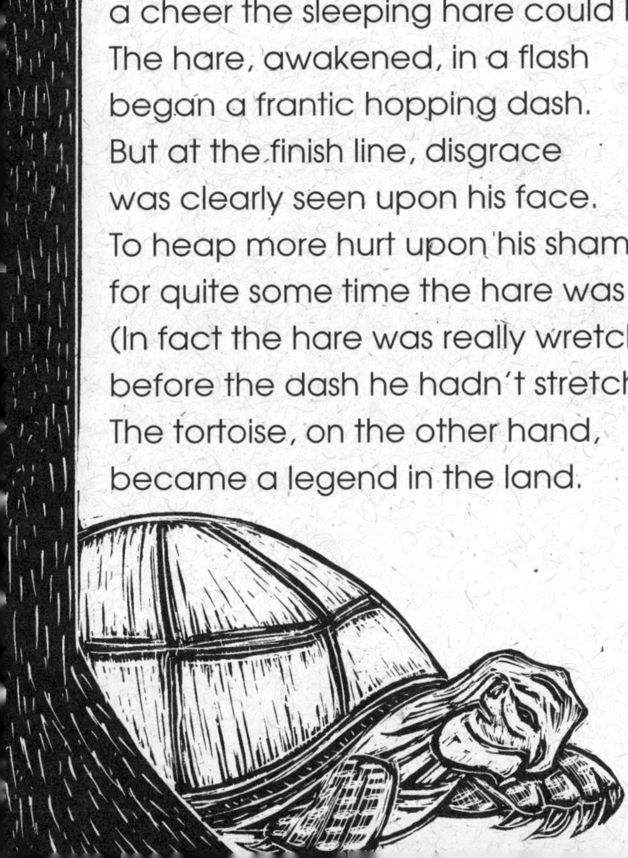

Scoffed Lion, "You're a scrawny sight.
You'd hardly make a decent bite."

Lion and Mouse

A mighty lion in his lair
slept peacefully without a care.
In fact, he dreamed of family feasts
on antelopes and wildebeests.
Abruptly ending Lion's doze,
a mouse ran right across his nose.
The lion, jarred, slammed down his paw,
and when he looked beneath, he saw
the little mouse, quite dazed and scared.
Yet, hoping that he might be spared,
the mouse, who had an active mind,
entreated, "If you were so kind
to let me go upon my way,
it just might be that I'd repay
your act of kindness. It could be
that sometime you'd need help from me."

Scoffed Lion, "You're a scrawny sight.
You'd hardly make a decent bite."
The lion, chuckling, set him free.
He wouldn't need this mouse, not he,
the king of beasts, so proud, so strong,
so self-sufficient, never wrong.

Watching Mousy run away
he called, "There simply is no way
you'd ever help me. To be blunt,
you drab, pathetic little runt,
your head's so teensy, weensy small,
there's hardly room for brains at all.
You have an ugly little tail.
It's naked, and it's thin and pale.
To boot, you've got black, beady eyes
and big buck teeth, twice normal size.
Your loudest sound's a silly squeak.
You'd be no help—you're much too weak."

Their lives went on much as before,
except, if Mousy heard a roar,
he listened, for he had to know,
was that the lion who'd let him go?
Mostly Mousy gathered seeds
and bits of fruits and tender weeds.
Lion hunted all night long,
then stretched out satisfied at dawn.

Not so many days passed by
when, suddenly, a lion's cry
alarmed the mouse one moonless night.
The mouse, concerned the lion might
just be the one he owed the debt,
discovered Lion in a net.

The lion thrashed, the lion screamed,
while from his eyes big teardrops streamed.
He saw the mouse, "Oh, I've been caught!
Is this my end? Is this my lot?
Two hunters trapped me in this net.
They've gone, but surely they will get
some help to drag me out of here,"
the lion bawled in frenzied fear.

The tiny mouse retained his wits;
he hadn't time for tizzy fits.
He knew he'd have to gnaw the net.
He didn't hesitate or fret.
At once the mouse began to gnaw.
His teeth were sharper than a saw.
You'd think that, maybe, in a flick,
the edges would get dull and thick.
But, actually, mouse teeth are made
so gnawing hones them like a blade.

Mouse gave his all. He took no rest
for time was limited. The test,
the goal—to set the lion free—
was daunting for a mouse; but he,
a stalwart trouper, paid his debt.
He chewed right through that awful net.

The lion, freed, escaped at last,
though none too soon, for very fast
the hunters came. They were too late.
A promise kept had cheated fate.

The bird convinced herself that she should help, especially for a fee.

Wolf and Crane

Soon after a tremendous meal,
a nasty wolf began to feel
some pain. For, due to sheer bad luck,
down in his throat a bone was stuck.
He took a drink. That made it worse.
He, naturally, began to curse.
Now, what he said was really bad.
Here's a cleaned-up version: "Gad-
zooks, old cheese, and smell of goat!
A blasted bone's plugged up my throat!"

When he could see that didn't help,
he then began to moan and yelp.
Such sounds of awful, piteous pain
were noticed by a distant crane.
Stretching to her greatest height,
the crane could glimpse the wolf's sad plight.
The wolf was writhing on the ground.
Now and then a gurgling sound
escaped from deep inside his jaws,
which he held clutched with both front paws.

Now cranes, it should be very clear,
regard a wolf with dread and fear.
The bone that caused the wolf to groan
could very well have been her own.
Nonetheless, she took to flight,
alighting well within his sight.

(Seeing her, Wolf thought, "What luck!
Her bill might reach the bone that's stuck.")

"Please, would you help? A bone is caught
deep in my throat. That bill you've got
is long and slim, and I've no doubt
that you could reach and pull it out."

The crane replied, "Now, let's be real—
I might become an easy meal
as soon as I relieve your pain.
For me it's all a risk—no gain."

The wolf replied with practiced guile,
"I'll even make it worth your while.
For any help you give to me,
I promise you'll receive a fee."

(I've never read that any cranes
had logical or clever brains.)

The bird convinced herself that she
should help, especially for a fee.
She carefully approached the beast,
not wishing to become his feast.
His actions could, of course, be fake.
Her tall, thin legs commenced to quake.

"Wolf," she ordered, "open wide!"
She craned her neck to peek inside,
then stuck her bill right down his jaw.
She got the jitters when she saw
the wolf's enormous canine teeth
and then his watering gums beneath.
His whiskers tickled both her eyes.
She questioned if this act were wise,
but, steadying her shaking knees,
the crane removed the bone with ease.
Instantly the crane leapt back
to guard herself against attack.

The wolf, relieved, said, "Thanks so much
for using such a gentle touch."
But when the crane asked, "Where's my fee?"
The wolf snapped back, "But you are free!"
He snarled, and his teeth were bared,
"Don't complain—your life was spared.
I didn't eat you—that's your fee.
What more did you expect from me?
You must be hopelessly obtuse.
The fee was nothing but a ruse.
And if you thought I'd keep my word,
you truly are a foolish bird."

The crane took wing, and off she flew,
for that was all she'd get, she knew.

He hopped up to the pitcher's lip,
rocked forward in his practiced dip,
but found his beak—indeed, the tip—
just couldn't reach. He got no sip.

Crow and the Pitcher

Listen, there goes Mr. Crow,
a bird that you might like to know.
Although his caw is rather gruff,
do not be fooled. The feathery fluff
and raucous call seem rather plain,
but he's got spirit and a brain.
Here's a story often heard
about this smart, persistent bird.

In summer, when the streams were dry,
the crow was searching from up high
for water, just to quench his thirst.
And though his eyes were good, at first,
from too high up, he couldn't see
the object near an olive tree,
a clear glass pitcher with some water
left there by a farmer's daughter.

The pitcher on that sunny day
caused a prism-like array
of rainbows of refracted light
attracting Mr. Crow. The sight

of water got him so excited,
he stubbed one toe when he alighted.
"Drat that pebble! Blast that stone!"
he cawed, then made a birdy groan.

He hopped up to the pitcher's lip,
rocked forward in his practiced dip,
but found his beak—indeed the tip—
just couldn't reach. He got no sip.
Said he, his wings upon his hips,
"This stinks! This hurts! This really rips!"

Soon Crow regained his normal cool,
for well he knew that only a fool
gives up so fast. "My throat's so dry.
I have to find a way. I'll try
to push the pitcher on its side,
then reach the water just inside."
Crow pushed that jug with all his might.
There was no movement, even slight.

"Now, since that bright ideas's shot,
I'll need another one," he thought.
He cocked his head, perused the ground.
His eyes homed in on something round—
the pebble that had hurt his toe.
"By golly, let's give this a go.

It wouldn't be a great surprise
if pebbles make the water rise.
I'll drop one in, this very one."
Instantly, Crow had begun.
He waited for the stone to sink,
and jumped up ready for his drink.
He got no drink. That raised his ire.
The water, though, seemed somewhat higher.
He persevered. Crow used his head.
Searching in a dry stream bed,
he found more pebbles. As he'd done,
he added pebbles, one by one.
At first he waited 'til they sank,
and he could hear a little clank.
But soon, of course, he'd drop and fly,
intent on raising the water high
enough so he could drink his fill.
Now and then he'd stick his bill
down in the pitcher for a test.
Then off he'd go without a rest.

As this became a tedious bore
he made a rhyme about his chore.
"Picky, pecky, pokey, peek.
Take a pebble in your beak.
Just above the jar below,
aim with care, and let it go!"

Finally, following one large stone,
he thought the water's height had grown
enough for him to have a sip.
He hopped upon the pitcher's lip,
and, with a happy gurgle, drank
so heartily that, to be frank,
it was by far his best drink ever—
this crow's reward for being clever.

The lesson from the crow's endeavor—
Don't quit! Keep trying! Don't say never!

. . . its leg held tightly in a snare
set by hunters with deadly care.

Repayment in Kind

In terraced fields where barley grew
among the olive trees, the view
so pleased the farmer that he stood
a moment. Movement in the distant wood—
a flutter—caught his careful eye,
and then he heard an eagle cry.
He hurried quickly to the spot
and found an eagle had been caught,
its leg held tightly in a snare
set by hunters with deadly care.
Now, truthfully, an eagle preys
upon the lambs that farmers raise.
A handsome bird, this eagle, though
a predator, seemed less a foe
than some majestic creature who
should soar above in skies of blue.
Besides, the farmer understood
that left, the eagle surely would
be killed. The eagle sensed its fate.
Yet, even in this fearful state,
the clever eagle cocked its head,
and by its soft look, truly said,

"Please free me. There may be a day
when such a kindness I'd repay."

The farmer thought, "It can't be wrong
to free this handsome eagle—strong
and beautiful, with amber eyes
so sharp, so reasoning, so wise."

With care the farmer set it free.
The eagle flew first to a tree
and then put on a flying show,
did somersaults—three in a row.
It dove, then climbed, then soaring high,
it dipped its wings to say goodbye.
The farmer knew he'd made a friend,
but thought this tie would quickly end.
Back he went to tend his crops,
for farmers' work just never stops.

A few months later, harvest in,
the farmer, who was tired and thin,
had spent the morning on repair
of terrace walls, for here and there
they crumbled. It took constant care
to keep ahead of age and wear.

The farmer sat against a wall,
when, suddenly, an eagle call
alerted him. And while he sat
the eagle snatched the farmer's hat.
The man jumped up in hot pursuit.
The eagle dropped its stolen loot.
The man let out an angry shout,
then noticed, when he turned about,
the wall had crumbled where he sat.
And, had he not pursued his hat,
he'd be beneath the broken wall.
Once more he heard the eagle call.
The farmer saw the bird above.
Wanting to express his love,
the farmer tried a backward flip.
(It hurt a bit—he bit his lip.)
And then he somersaulted twice,
plus, just to add a bit of spice,
he cartwheeled clear around the field.
Then, in thankfulness, he kneeled.

The eagle watched the man's display,
then dipped its wings as if to say,
"A kind deed was repaid today."
Majestically it flew away.